Puppy

Playtime for Rascal

Gulp!

For Tom ~ H.W.
For Fi and Morris ~ K.P.

WOOF

magazine

STRIPES PUBLISHING
An imprint of Magi Publications
1 The Coda Centre,
189 Munster Road,
London SW6 6AW

A paperback original
First published in Great Britain
in 2010

Text copyright © Holly Webb, 2010
Illustrations copyright
© Kate Pankhurst, 2010
Cover photographs copyright
© Lifeonwhite.com, 2010

ISBN: 978-1-84715-136-0

The right of Holly Webb and Kate
Pankhurst to be identified as the
author and illustrator of this work
respectively has been asserted by
them in accordance with the
Copyright, Designs and Patents
Act, 1988.

A CIP catalogue record for this
book is available from the British
Library.

Printed and bound in the UK.

10 9 8 7 6 5 4 3 2 1

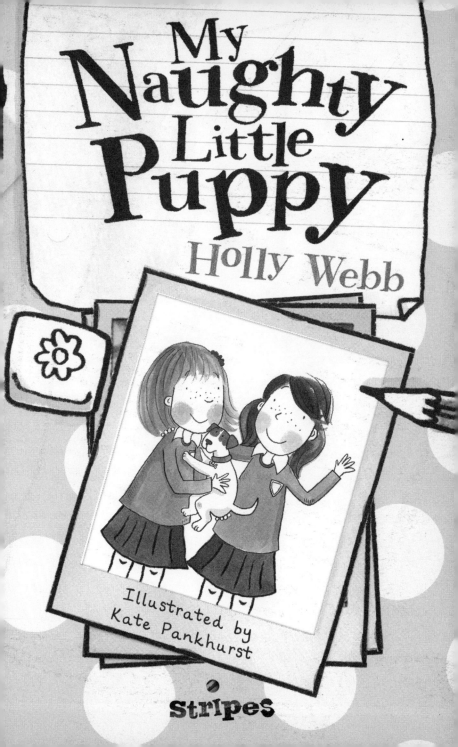

My Naughty Little Puppy

Holly Webb

Illustrated by
Kate Pankhurst

Stripes

Chapter One

Frisbee Fun

"Go on, Ellie! Chase it!" Max shouted. "Just jump up and grab the Frisbee!"

Ellie did her best, racing across the grass, but Max had thrown the bright yellow Frisbee as hard as he could, and it was curving round. She looked behind her anxiously, trying to see where it would land.

"Wrong way!" Lila yelled, starting to dash after the Frisbee too. "Ellie, you can get it if you run!"

My Naughty Little Puppy

Ellie could hear Max behind her, muttering about how useless she was, and her cheeks went pink. Why did her older brother and sister have to be so sporty? Max took it all so seriously too, when it was only meant to be fun!

Then she started to giggle. Rascal, her Jack Russell puppy, was galloping after the Frisbee too.

He launched himself into the air and grabbed the Frisbee in his jaws, while he was half a metre off the ground. He landed on all four paws, looking very pleased with himself.

"Wow, Ellie, your dog's a lot better at catching than you," Max teased. "Here, Rascal, give it up, boy."

My Naughty Little Puppy

Rascal looked up at Max, the Frisbee hanging out of his mouth. It was almost as big as he was, and his shiny black eyes sparkled over the top of it. He shook his head wildly, swinging the Frisbee back and forth.

"I think he might be trying to kill your Frisbee, Max." Lila giggled.

Max bent down and grasped the Frisbee – but Rascal came with it, hanging on by his teeth.

"Put him down, Max, you'll hurt his mouth!" Ellie cried. "Rascal, come on, let's play some more. Give it to me!"

Back on the ground, Rascal eyed Ellie thoughtfully, and spat out the Frisbee into her hand. Then he stood there wagging his

My Naughty Little Puppy

tail hopefully and staring up at them.

Max grinned. "OK, Rascal, this one's for you, boy!" He flicked his wrist, sending the Frisbee curving out over the grass. Rascal hurled himself after it.
He managed to grab it just as it was about to hit the ground, and then scampered back, dragging it along behind him in his teeth.

"He's so good!" Lila said, and Ellie glowed with pride. Her older brother and sister loved Rascal, but they spent a lot of time moaning about how naughty he was. Rascal was a monster for chewing things, shoes especially.

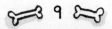

My Naughty Little Puppy

"That was excellent," Max said, as
Rascal trotted off, the Frisbee still in his
mouth. "We just need to explain to Rascal
that he's supposed to give the Frisbee
back..."

Ellie told her best friend Christy all about
the Frisbee session at school on Monday.
"Have you ever tried playing Frisbee with
Bouncer?" she asked. Bouncer was
Christy's gorgeous Labrador.

Christy looked thoughtful. "He's ace at
fetching, but he only really likes chasing
sticks."

"It was really funny." Ellie laughed.
"Rascal turned himself right over in the air to

get one catch." She put her chin on her hands. "It stopped Max and Lila moaning about how bad I was at catching it, anyway. I wish I was better at sporty things!"

Christy shook her head. "You can't be good at everything, Ellie! You're an arty person."

Mrs Harley finished the register. "Now for some exciting news, everybody. Mr Turner's just been telling all the staff about Sports Day!"

Ellie stared at Mrs Harley in horror. Sports Day! She'd almost forgotten it would be that time of year soon. "Oh, no..." she murmured.

Christy put her hand over her mouth, trying not to laugh. "Sorry!" she whispered.

My Naughty Little Puppy

"But it is funny that you've just been saying
how much you hate sporty stuff!"

"So over this week and next week, we'll
be doing lots of Sports Day practice," Mrs
Harley went on. "And this year, with the
Olympics coming up soon, we've got a
special project too!"

Ellie looked up at their teacher
anxiously. Not more sporty things?

My Naughty Little Puppy

"I'd like you to create something really special round the theme of the Olympics. It could be a piece of writing, a painting, some music – whatever you like."

Christy stuck her hand in the air. "Mrs Harley, can we do it together?"

Mrs Harley nodded. "No more than three in a group though, please. And your project needs to be handed in next Thursday, the day before Sports Day. Then Mr Turner will pick the best one from each year, and they'll be on display at Sports Day."

Ellie looked at her friend hopefully. At least Christy was sporty! If they did their project together, it might not be so bad... It was just a shame they couldn't team up for Sports Day!

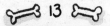 13

Chapter Two

Ellie's Sporty Plan

Mum brought Rascal with her when she came to pick up Ellie. Max was staying for football and getting a lift later, and Christy was coming home with them for tea.

"We can start on the project!" Christy said excitedly.

Ellie pulled a face.

"What's the matter?" Mum asked. "What sort of project is it?"

"A sporty one." Ellie sighed. "Because it's

going to be Sports Day at the end of next week. We've got a note asking if you want to come and watch. You don't, do you?"

"Of course I do!" Mum gave her a sympathetic smile. "Are you really not looking forward to it?"

Ellie shuddered. "You can watch Max. I don't want anyone watching me come last at everything."

"You won't!" Mum laughed.

Ellie gave her a look. She had the year before - it had been awful.

"But it isn't really a sporty project," Christy put in. "It just has to be about the Olympics. Maybe we could do a comic about it. I'll write and you can draw."

Ellie nodded. "That sounds quite fun."

My Naughty Little Puppy

"Or we could make a model?"

"Oooh, yes!" exclaimed Ellie.

Rascal looked up, his tail wagging madly. The girls' voices were making him feel jumpy and excited, and he suddenly shot off down the road, pulling Ellie along with him.

My Naughty Little Puppy

Ellie raced behind him, panting, "Rascal, stop!" But he didn't, not until they reached the corner, where there was a good lamp post to sniff. Then he looked up at her, his dark eyes glinting naughtily.

"You can run really fast when you've got Rascal pulling you!" said Christy, as she caught Ellie up. "Maybe you should ask Mrs Harley if we can have a race with our dogs at Sports Day."

Ellie looked down at Rascal thoughtfully. She couldn't see Mrs Harley agreeing to that, but perhaps Rascal could help her to practise. He was definitely better at running and catching things than she was!

My Naughty Little Puppy

"So what kind of model shall we make?" Ellie asked, setting out her drawing things on her desk. She looked down at Christy, who was sitting on the floor, tickling Rascal.

"You tell me!" said Christy. "I know it's a sports project, but you're the one that's brilliant at making things."

"We could make the Olympic stadium in London," Ellie suggested. "I've got some sheets of card; they were in this fab craft kit that Auntie Gemma gave me."

"That's a great idea," said Christy, jumping to her feet. "Let's ask your mum if we can look up the stadium on the net."

A few minutes later, Christy and Ellie were staring at the computer screen in Ellie's mum's little office under the stairs.

Christy wrinkled her nose. "You're sure if we make a model of that it won't just look like a huge doughnut?" she asked.

Ellie shook her head. "Not if we paint it all silver."

"Your tea's ready, girls!" Mum called from the kitchen.

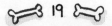

My Naughty Little Puppy

Max had just got home from football and was sitting at the table looking hungry, as the girls came in with Rascal trotting after them.

"Heard about Sports Day?" he asked Ellie, smirking. He loved Sports Day, and usually won at least two races.

Ellie went pink. "Yes," she muttered. The look on Max's face made her even more determined to practise with Rascal. She was going to try and win something this year! Or at least not be last...

Lila wandered in reading a magazine. "Hello, Christy... Oh, have you got Sports Day, Ellie? They ought to do dancing and things as well, it's totally unfair on people who don't like running."

Ellie nodded. She definitely agreed.

My Naughty Little Puppy

"Hey!" Christy squeaked, making Ellie
jump. "Where did my sausage go?"

Ellie leaned down to look under the
table. Rascal looked back at
her and gave a huge
gulp, the last of Christy's
sausage disappearing
swiftly between his white
teeth. He eyed her guiltily.

"Sorry, Christy! You can have mine, go
on. How did he even get up there without
us noticing?" Ellie asked.

Lila shrugged. "He must have jumped
on to Dad's chair, and just popped his nose
up and grabbed it. He's a monster. Do you
want some of my beans, Ellie, if Christy's
having your sausage?"

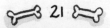

My Naughty Little Puppy

"Yes, please." Ellie peered back under the table. "Rascal, you're a piglet!" Then she smiled to herself. He needed to keep his strength up for running!

Back up in her room, while they were drawing a plan for their model Olympic stadium, Ellie told Christy her idea to practise for Sports Day with Rascal.

"That's a brilliant idea!" cried Christy. "Can me and Bouncer join in, too? We could all go to the park on Saturday."

"That would be fun," Ellie replied. But secretly she planned to practise in her garden before Saturday as well, so as to make sure she didn't disgrace herself.

Chapter Three

The Big Dog Race

"What's Ellie doing out there with Rascal?" Grandad asked, staring out of the kitchen window into the garden.

Mum came over to look. "Oh! She's preparing for Sports Day. She's been practising with Rascal all week."

Out in the garden, Ellie and Rascal raced up to the lilac tree and back. As Ellie reached the patio, she looked up and spotted Grandad. She waved and trailed

over to the kitchen door, Rascal trotting
behind her. Even *he* looked tired.

"Working hard for Sports Day then?"
Grandad asked, as he gave her a hug.

Ellie nodded. "I just want to get a bit
faster. And we've been practising welly-
throwing too – that's one of the events."

"Don't you get to practise at school?"
Grandad asked.

My Naughty Little Puppy

"Oh, yes!" Ellie went pink. "But at school I get really nervous because everyone's watching, and that makes me even worse."

Grandad nodded. "I'm sure practising will help. But it's not the end of the world if you don't win, you know. I was never a very fast runner. I got better at it as I grew though. Perhaps when you get a bit taller, Ellie."

Ellie sighed. That was all very well, but she wasn't going to get any taller by next Friday...

"Anyway, I've got a present – look! A new lead for Rascal. It's an extendable one, so you can go running in the park with him."

Ellie beamed and gave him a hug. "Thanks, Grandad! I'm going to the park with Christy tomorrow, we can try it out then."

My Naughty Little Puppy

"Rascal, stop pulling or I'll drop everything!" Ellie was trying to hold Rascal, and carry all the stuff she'd brought for their Sports Day practice at the park. Of course, Rascal had chosen that moment to forget about walking to heel. It didn't help that he was on his special new lead. It was very clever – the plastic handle had a lead inside that pulled out to eight metres long! Ellie was finding it a bit tricky though, because if she pressed the button by mistake it extended when she didn't mean it to.

"Here, I'll take the water bottles." Christy grabbed them just before they slipped out of Ellie's arms.

"Thanks! Oh, I'm glad
we're here," Ellie said, as they
went through the park gates. She put down
the rest of her things and gazed round the
park. Lots of people were doing sporty
stuff. A couple of girls were rollerblading,
and there was a man in luminous yellow
trainers jogging along the path.

Rascal growled quietly, and Ellie looked
down at him. "What's up, Rascal?"

My Naughty Little Puppy

"I think it's that jogger," Christy whispered. "I don't think Rascal likes his trainers!"

Ellie crouched down to stroke Rascal and tell him it was OK, but Rascal wasn't paying attention. His lips were lifting back from his teeth as he growled, making him look really fierce. As the jogger ran past them on the path, he suddenly barked

My Naughty Little Puppy

loudly and shot after him. Ellie dropped the
plastic handle of his lead, and then
grabbed it again with a sigh of relief - but
the button must have banged on the path,
and the extending part started to unroll.

"Oh, no!" Ellie gasped, as Rascal set off
after the jogger and his trainers, barking
wildly. "Rascal, come back," she called out,
chasing after him.

My Naughty Little Puppy

The man looked round, and his eyebrows shot up in surprise. He started to run faster, but Rascal was gaining on him.

Ellie was trailing behind them. Then she came to a stop, realizing that chasing Rascal just meant that he could chase the jogger! She set her feet firmly on the path, grabbed a handful of the extending lead, and tried to reel Rascal back in. Rascal yelped in surprise.

The jogger put on a burst of speed and disappeared out of the park gates, casting a grumpy look at Ellie over his shoulder.

"I'm so embarrassed!" Ellie hissed to Christy, as she joined her and Bouncer.

Christy giggled. "It was definitely those trainers that caught his attention."

My Naughty Little Puppy

Rascal glared at the gate, as though he thought the jogger might come back.

"Look at it this way," Christy told Ellie. "You were running really fast!"

Ellie sighed and stared out across the park. Just then, she spotted a boy whose dog was almost as big as he was. "Oh, look, Rascal, it's Jack and Hugo!" She waved, and the boy waved back. Ellie turned to Christy. "That's Jack, our friend from puppy-training. He's the one with the Great Dane, look, over by the swings."

Christy's mouth dropped open. "But that dog is *huge*! He can't still be a puppy!"

"Hi, Jack!" Ellie called, as Jack and Hugo loped over to them. "This is my best friend Christy, and her dog, Bouncer."

Hugo and Rascal sniffed each other in a friendly sort of way, and Bouncer eyed Hugo carefully. Bouncer probably wasn't used to being the smaller dog, Ellie thought, but then anything was small compared to Hugo.

"Hi, Christy." Jack smiled, then looked at the welly in the girls' pile of stuff. "Why have you only got one welly?" he asked. "Has Rascal been eating shoes again?"

My Naughty Little Puppy

Ellie laughed. "No, we've come to the park to practise for our school Sports Day," she explained. "One of the events is welly-throwing." She didn't add that welly-throwing was the one competition she thought she might have a chance to do well in. She didn't find it easy to get the welly in quite the right place, but hopefully no one else would have practised as much as she was going to.

"But Rascal is still mad on shoes," she added. "Look." She showed him the welly, which was chewed all round the top. "Mum says it still keeps the water out, so there's no way she's getting me new ones."

"You're very keen, doing extra practice," Jack said, and Ellie went pink.

My Naughty Little Puppy

"Christy's really good at sports, but I'm not," she explained quickly. "I run lots faster when I'm chasing after Rascal, though."

Jack grinned. "Cool. You've got a secret weapon. Can I join in? I think our Sports Day's later in the term, but it would be good to get ready."

Christy nodded. "Sure. We're going to do a running race, a skipping race and a sack race too." She pulled a black dustbin bag out of her rucksack. "I wanted to bring a pillowcase, but Mum said no, so this is the closest thing I could find to a sack."

Ellie took out a skipping rope from her bag. "We can use this to make the circle to throw the welly in," she explained.

Jack grinned. "You should have brought

the other welly, to give Rascal something to chew on while he's watching."

"Let's start with running," Christy suggested. "How about from here to that lamp post? That's a hundred metres, ish." Christy gave Ellie a stern look. "Stop looking so worried! Just pretend you're out walking with Rascal and he's seen a squirrel!"

"OK." Ellie nodded, and the three of them lined up. The dogs looked around excitedly, wondering what was going on.

"Ready, steady, go!" Christy yelled, and she shot off really fast, Bouncer galloping beside her.

"Come on, Rascal!" Ellie called, and Rascal gave a sharp yap and scampered

My Naughty Little Puppy

after Bouncer. Hugo launched himself across the grass, and with his long legs he soon overtook Rascal, who went into a frenzy of barking. Then Hugo overtook Bouncer, too.

My Naughty Little Puppy

Ellie reached the lamp post last, and sighed.

"You weren't last by much at all!" Christy said encouragingly, as the three of them sat down on the grass. "I wouldn't have thought such a huge dog could run so fast, Jack. Hugo's amazing!"

Jack patted Hugo proudly, as the big dog lay down next to him, panting. "He is, isn't he?"

"But you should have seen Ellie running with Rascal earlier..." said Christy to Jack, giving Ellie a wink.

Chapter Four

Rascal the Magazine Muncher

"Can we practise the welly-throwing now?" Ellie said, getting to her feet. Jack had finally stopped laughing at Christy's story of Rascal and the jogger with the luminous yellow trainers.

Rascal looked interested as she picked up the welly. "It isn't for you!" Ellie told him sternly, and he flattened his ears. "Oh, it's OK, I'm not cross. But you can't chew it any more, it'll be no use as a welly soon."

My Naughty Little Puppy

She laid the skipping rope out in a circle and paced back carefully. They'd been practising this at school, so she knew how far away she ought to be.

"Let me take Rascal's lead while you throw," Christy offered. "I'll take him over here away from the welly – he's definitely eyeing it up."

Ellie looked at the target and started to swing the welly. She shut her eyes for a second, and then opened them and let go.

The welly didn't hit the skipping-rope target, but that was because the target wasn't there any more. Neither were Christy and Rascal. They were halfway across the park, with the skipping-rope trailing out of Rascal's mouth and wrapped around his paws.

"Sorry!" Christy called back. "He surprised me; I thought he was going for the welly!"

Ellie sighed and looked at Jack, who was leaning against Hugo and practically crying with laughter.

"At least puppy-training starts again on Monday," he said. "I think Rascal needs it."

My Naughty Little Puppy

Ellie was looking forward to puppy-training. She and Rascal had already done the beginners' class, which was where they'd met Jack and Hugo, and now they were all signed up for the next set of lessons, where they would do more complicated things.

"Honestly, Rascal. I think Jack's right," Ellie told him, shaking her head, as they walked round the corner to her house after saying goodbye to Christy. "What are you like? Dogs aren't supposed to chase skipping ropes!"

Ellie put out some food for Rascal when she got home and then went upstairs. She flopped on to her bed and admired the model stadium that was sitting on her desk. She and Christy had been working on it

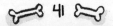

almost every afternoon after school, and it was very fiddly. They'd used up three boxes of toothpicks making the metal struts round the outside of the building. Now all Ellie had to do was spray-paint it silver – Mum was going to get some silver paint on Monday – and then stick on figures of athletes inside the arena. She'd already made those, but they had to wait until the silver paint was dry. Christy was cutting out hundreds of tiny pictures of people from catalogues and magazines, so that they could stick them into the audience. It was going to be brilliant when it was finished!

My Naughty Little Puppy

"Ellieeee! Look what Rascal's done this time!" Max was yelling from downstairs. Ellie groaned and rushed out on to the landing. He'd only been alone for a few minutes...

Max stomped up the stairs. He had Rascal under one arm and a magazine in his hand.

"What's the matter?" Ellie asked.

"I only bought it this morning!" Max scowled. "My new athletics magazine! I wanted to get some training tips out of it for Sports Day. Look at it now!" He shook it open. The magazine had been chewed to pieces.

My Naughty Little Puppy

"Oh, Rascal!" Ellie said with a sigh.

Rascal stretched out and gave the magazine an interested sniff. Max snatched it back out of his reach at once. "All I did was put it down on the sofa!" he said crossly.

"I'll ask Mum if I can go down to the newsagent's and buy you a new one," Ellie promised.

"Thanks," Max muttered grumpily. He thrust Rascal into her arms and disappeared into his room.

Ellie eyed Rascal sternly. "Don't give me that cheeky look. I have to buy Max another magazine now, out of my pocket money, which means no more special marrowbone treats for you this week!"

Chapter Five

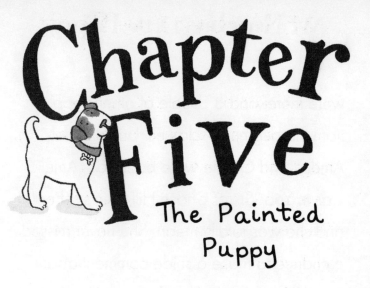

The Painted Puppy

Ellie was really pleased to see Jo, their puppy-training instructor, again on Monday night. Jo had given her loads of useful tips for looking after Rascal. She smiled to herself as she walked into the village hall with Dad and Rascal, wondering if Jo could teach her how to stop Rascal stealing skipping ropes and chewing magazines...

Jo nodded hello as all the owners and puppies formed a circle. Jack and Hugo

were there, and a couple of other people from the beginners' classes. Unfortunately, Amelia and Goldie were back, too. Amelia was in Year Six at Chase Hill, Ellie's school, and she was totally mean. She never missed a chance to make a snide comment about Rascal or Hugo. When she saw Ellie and her dad walking in, she actually groaned. Ellie went pink, but ignored her.

Jo explained that she was going to teach the dogs to come back properly when they were called, so that it was safe for them to be let off the lead.

"That means we'll be able to teach the puppies to fetch properly too," she pointed out. "It's great exercise for your dogs, and loads of fun."

My Naughty Little Puppy

Ellie smiled when she heard that. Rascal had been so good at fetching the Frisbee in the garden. But she hadn't yet dared to let him off the lead anywhere else. She was never quite sure if he'd come back. So it sounded as though these classes were going to be just what he needed.

They had a game of fetch at the end of the class. Jo had brought along some soft beanbags, which wouldn't go bouncing off all round the hall like balls would.

"Remember we want the puppies to give the beanbags back to you, with no pulling or growling," Jo said, as she handed them out. "They might find that a bit tricky at first, so don't worry if they don't get it straight away."

My Naughty Little Puppy

Ellie frowned, remembering Rascal with
Max's Frisbee. But maybe it would be OK.
She threw the beanbag and called,
"Rascal, fetch!" He raced off instantly,
whisking the beanbag from the floor.

Smiling to herself, Ellie reached for the
beanbag as Rascal dashed back to her.
"Drop it, Rascal!" But Rascal shook the
beanbag, wagging his tail happily. Why
on earth would he want to give up such a
fun toy? Ellie tugged it gently – and Rascal
tugged back.

My Naughty Little Puppy

Suddenly, the beanbag split down the seam, sending beans cascading all over the floor. Rascal stood in the middle of the mess and gave Ellie a look, as if to say it was all her fault...

Grandad was at Ellie's house when she, Dad and Rascal got back.

"How was your class, Ellie?" he asked, giving her a hug.

"It was great. We're teaching the puppies how to fetch," Ellie explained. "Rascal's really good at it, except the bit where he's supposed to give what he's fetched back to me. Oh, thanks, Mum," she said, as Mum poured her a glass of milk.

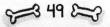

My Naughty Little Puppy

Puppy-training had made her thirsty. She told Grandad all about the beanbag disaster. "But Jo said it didn't matter, they were really old beanbags."

Grandad laughed. "And your mum says you've been working on a special project for school. May I see it?"

Ellie nodded eagerly. "You'll have to come upstairs. Christy came round straight after school, and we spray-painted it. It's still sticky, though."

Mum looked up. "Oh, Ellie, I opened your bedroom door and your window – the smell of that paint was very strong. I wanted to air the room before you go to bed. Leave your door open when you come back down, please."

My Naughty Little Puppy

Ellie nodded, and led Grandad upstairs to show off her model. "Urrgh, you can smell the paint all the way from here," she murmured, wrinkling her nose. "Look, it's on my desk," she said proudly, pushing her door wide open.

Grandad caught his breath, and Ellie looked over at her desk, expecting him to comment on the amazing model.

Then she gasped. Her and Christy's beautiful stadium was lying squashed on her desk, and there was a small, silvery-patched dog sitting in the middle of it.

My Naughty Little Puppy

"Christy's going to be so cross! And Rascal's going to be silver for ever!" Ellie wailed. She was sitting on the kitchen floor, holding Rascal, while Mum and Grandad tried to wipe the paint off his coat.

Dad rushed into the kitchen, waving a bottle. "The vet's advice line said it wouldn't be poisonous, and to try washing it out with mild baby shampoo."

"We'll get it off, Ellie," Grandad said, as Mum started to fill the kitchen sink with water. "It's only in patches, not all over him."

Ellie nodded, but tears were still trickling out of the corners of her eyes as she lifted Rascal into the sink.

My Naughty Little Puppy

"Oh, Rascal, hold still!" Mum cried, as
he sent a surge of water all over the floor.
"We're trying to help, you silly dog!"

"It's coming off, I think," Ellie said
doubtfully, peering at the sticky silvery
patches, and Mum nodded.

"About time too, this nail brush is never
going to be the same again."

My Naughty Little Puppy

Ellie sighed. She still had to tell Christy their model was ruined. She lifted Rascal out of the sink and wrapped him in the old towel that Mum had given her. He snuggled against her, warm and damp, and licked her ear lovingly. "Can I go and ring Christy?" she gulped.

Mum glanced at the clock. "It's a bit late, Ellie. I expect she'll be in bed by now." She put a wet arm around Ellie and Rascal. "Tell her at school tomorrow."

Ellie nodded and set Rascal down on the floor to dry him.

Grandad reached out and patted her shoulder. "She'll understand, love," he murmured, but Ellie could feel herself starting to cry again.

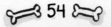

"We did such a lot of work, and it's all wasted! I should have put the model somewhere safe, but I just forgot!"

"It's my fault for leaving your door open." Mum sighed. "I didn't think either. All those times I've told you to be careful."

Rascal looked up at Ellie anxiously and whined. Tears were dropping on to his nose.

My Naughty Little Puppy

"You've still got those figures you painted," Dad reminded her. "And the bits that Christy's got at her house."

Ellie glanced up. "But the building part's all ruined," she sniffed. "We just don't have time to make it again. And Christy's going to be really upset."

Grandad handed Ellie a tissue. "Christy's a good friend. I know she'll be upset, but she'll come round. You're so good at making things, you and Christy will think of something."

Ellie nodded and dried her eyes. She just hoped Grandad was right.

Chapter Six

Breaking the News

Ellie yawned sleepily and rolled over, glad that it wasn't time to get up yet. Then the little ball of fur on the end of her bed wriggled and squeaked in his sleep, and Ellie woke up a bit more. The sun was shining through the crack in the curtains, and in the half-light she could see the silvery patch on Rascal's back that they hadn't quite been able to get out.

Ellie sat up and gazed over at her desk

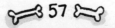

- the model looked awful. How was she ever going to tell Christy? If only she'd put it on top of her bookshelf to dry. And if only Mum hadn't worried so much about the paint smell!

Ellie looked over at her clock. She might as well get up, it was half-past six anyway. Maybe there was something she could do to rescue the model.

But when Mum came in to wake Ellie up, she found her sitting at her desk, still trying to untangle a mess of silver-painted toothpicks.

"Oh, dear. He really squashed it thoroughly, didn't he?"

Ellie nodded. "I'm just going to have to start again."

My Naughty Little Puppy

"Why don't you invite Christy round tonight after school to help?" Mum said.

"I wish I didn't have to go to school," Ellie muttered. But she knew she had to.

Christy was waiting by the school gates as usual, and as soon as Ellie saw her, her heart started to thud.

"What's the matter?" Christy asked, when she saw Ellie's worried face.

Ellie gulped. "Rascal ruined our model!" she gabbled out.

Christy stared at her. "What – the whole thing?" she whispered.

Ellie nodded miserably. "I tried to fix it this morning, but it's still a mess. I'm so sorry."

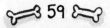

My Naughty Little Puppy

"Oh, Ellie! All that work," Christy cried.
"We spent ages on it!" She looked up
crossly. "I wish you'd teach Rascal to
behave! He really is a monster!"

Ellie felt as though she was going to cry.
She didn't even try to stand up for Rascal
like she normally would. He was a monster!

She started to say sorry all over again,
but then the bell rang, and Christy stomped
off into school, leaving her behind.

My Naughty Little Puppy

Ellie watched her go, her eyes filling with tears. She'd known Christy would be furious, but they hardly ever had fights, and it was horrible. She had to stop crying before anybody came to ask her what was wrong. She dried her eyes on her sleeve and walked slowly into class.

Christy was already at their table when Ellie got in. Ellie glanced at her nervously as she put away her bag, wondering whether she should try and move seats. But Christy looked up as she walked over to the desk.

"Sorry I yelled at you," Christy murmured. "I know you're training Rascal, and he's not really a monster. What happened?"

Ellie gave a little sigh of relief and sat down. "Mum left my bedroom door open, because of the smell of the paint... Are you really, really cross?" she added in a whisper. Luckily, Mrs Harley was busy dealing with someone's forgotten homework and hadn't spotted them talking.

Christy shook her head. "No. Well, I am. But it's like when I spilled chocolate milkshake over your favourite T-shirt. I didn't mean to, and neither did you this time. I don't suppose you've thought about glueing Rascal's teeth together, though?" She grinned.

"The silver paint nearly did that. He was covered in it. Dad had to ring the vet to find out what to do."

Christy giggled. "What are we going to do? We've only got two days till we have to hand in the project."

"Mum says you can come round tonight so we can make something new."

Christy frowned. "OK. But maybe you'd better come to mine. I'm sure Mum will say yes. Then we can leave the model at my house. Bouncer doesn't really chew things." She crossed her fingers. "Well, not much, anyway..."

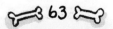

My Naughty Little Puppy

Ellie nodded. She was so glad Christy was still friends with her. "That would be great. I'll go home and pick up the figures I made. He didn't get at those. But I'd better take Rascal for a walk first. He gets even naughtier if he doesn't have any exercise."

"Why don't you bring him too? Then he can play with Bouncer in the garden," Christy suggested. "We can ban them both from my bedroom while we're making stuff."

"Rascal would love that. Bouncer and Hugo are his best friends." Ellie gave Christy a quick hug. "Thank you for being so nice! I thought you were going to go mad."

Christy grinned. "You owe me!"

Chapter Seven

Ellie's Brainwave

Christy and Ellie dashed out of school at home time to find their mums and ask if their plan for the evening was all right. Ellie's mum was showing Christy's mum the silvery patch on Rascal's back.

"Hello, girls!" Christy's mum smiled at them both, and gave Christy a hug. "Your mum told me what happened, Ellie. Don't worry, I'm sure we can sort something out."

My Naughty Little Puppy

"Can we start on the new model at ours tonight, Mum? As it's an emergency," Christy begged. "Please? Ellie can bring Rascal to play with Bouncer, then they'll both be busy and we can get on with making it."

"Fine with me." Christy's mum nodded.

"Good idea," Ellie's mum said.

"I'll go home and get the figures, and come round to yours. And I'll bring the card," Ellie added. Then her face crumpled. "Oh no, the card! We used it all up! There's only a few scraps left."

Christy bit her lip. "I didn't think of that. Is it too late to walk into town and go to the art shop?"

"I think it is," her mum said, looking at

her watch. "Can't you use something else?"

"I've got some craft stuff, but not much. We might need to make something different – not a whole stadium, I mean." Christy frowned.

Ellie nodded sadly. "It was such a cool idea. Well, I'll bring round what I've got left and we'll just have to do our best."

Ellie had Rascal's lead in one hand, and a bag of bits in the other. She'd gone through her room like a whirlwind, searching for anything that she could use for their model. Hopefully when they laid it all out at Christy's, it would give them a brainwave.

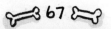

My Naughty Little Puppy

She was just ringing Christy's doorbell, when Rascal pulled on his lead. Christy's recycling box was overflowing, and Rascal started sniffing around it. "No, Rascal. That's rubbish, leave it alone."

Rascal ignored her and tried to tug out an interesting-smelling bit of cardboard with his teeth.

"Leave it, Rascal, we don't want it!" Then Ellie smiled. Cardboard! That was exactly what she wanted!

When Christy opened the door, she found Ellie on her knees rooting through the box, sorting out toilet roll tubes, cereal boxes, even plastic milk bottles.

"What are you doing? Did Rascal knock it over?" Christy asked.

"No, but look! We can make our stadium
out of the recycling!" Ellie told Christy, her
eyes sparkling. Rascal picked up a toilet roll
tube in his teeth and gave a muffled yap.

Christy sat down on the front step. "Are
you sure? It doesn't look like we could use
those bits to make the same shape."

Ellie beamed at her. "We don't have to.
We can design our own stadium!" She
screwed up her eyes as she thought.

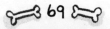

My Naughty Little Puppy

"Oh, and we could make it really
environmentally friendly, like in that project
we did last term. With a wind turbine on
the roof and rainwater harvesting!"

"That does sound good." Christy smiled.
"Can we build something so that when the
runners are training they're in a giant
hamster wheel thing and that generates
electricity to make all the lights go on?"

"Definitely." Ellie nodded. "We can
make that out of the toothpicks we had left
over from the last one. Will your mum mind
if we use all this? We'd better check."

Christy grabbed a handful of bits from the
recycling box, and they headed into the
kitchen to find Bouncer and let the two dogs
out into the garden. Bouncer pricked up his

ears as soon as he saw Rascal, and the pair of them chased off down the garden path.

Christy's mum was fine about them using the recycling. In fact, she thought it was a brilliant idea. The girls dashed upstairs, carrying all the bits of recycling, and a big plastic sheet that she'd given them so they could lay it all out without making a mess on the bedroom carpet.

An hour later, the stadium was taking shape. It still looked like a pile of cereal boxes, with towers made out of loo rolls, but Ellie could see that it was going to work. She was particularly proud of her egg box fold-away roof – it was lucky that Christy's dad loved to make himself scrambled eggs for breakfast!

Christy looked at it with her head on one side. "When it's sprayed silver, I think it'll look even better than the old one. And no one else will have a project like it."

The mention of silver paint reminded Ellie about Rascal. "I hope the dogs are still OK in the garden."

Christy jumped up and peered out of her window. "Well, Bouncer's asleep under the bench, I can see his tail sticking out. I can't see Rascal, though."

My Naughty Little Puppy

Ellie ran over to look as well. "I can't see him either. We'd better go and check, just in case..."

The girls hurried downstairs, and through the back door. Bouncer woke up as they came out and thumped his tail sleepily. But there was no sign of Rascal.

"Where can he be?" Ellie muttered, running down the path. "Rascal! Rascal!" She peered behind the shed, wondering if he'd gone digging – he loved to dig holes. But no muddy little dog poked his head out. "He must be here somewhere. He couldn't have escaped, could he?"

"No, there is a hole under the fence, but it isn't big enough..." Christy's eyes widened. "Oh, no. It's not big enough for Bouncer, but

My Naughty Little Puppy

Rascal could get through it!" She ran over to the wheelbarrow standing by the shed. "Help me push this to the fence so we can look over. Quietly!" she hissed. "Mr Simpson next door really hates dogs – he always complains that Bouncer barks too much."

They pushed the wheelbarrow up against the fence, and scrambled into it to peer over.

"Oh, no..." Christy gasped.

The garden on the other side of the fence was immaculate, as though every blade of grass had been measured. And snuffling around the rose bushes was a small brown and white (and silver) dog. Rascal looked up at them and wagged his tail happily.

My Naughty Little Puppy

"Rascal! Rascal, here!" Ellie tried to use the firm tone of voice that Jo had talked about at training, but it came out all high and worried, and Rascal ignored her.

"Shall I go and get some treats to tempt him with?" Christy suggested.

My Naughty Little Puppy

"Oi! What do you two think you're doing?" A loud yell echoed across the garden, as the neighbour's back door flew open and Mr Simpson tramped down the garden path. "What's that in my roses? Get out of there, you little menace!"

As the girls quickly tried to get down, the wheelbarrow wobbled, tipping them into a muddy patch of flower bed.

Mr Simpson stuck his head over the fence, and glared down at them.

My Naughty Little Puppy

Before he could say a word, Rascal shot through the gap under the fence, and bolted over to Ellie. He looked very scared. As Ellie scooped him up, he buried his head under her arm, quivering.

"That dog has just been *waltzing* through my rose bushes!" Mr Simpson roared.

"I'm really sorry," Christy squeaked. "We didn't realize he could get through the gap under the fence. He's just visiting..."

"Hmph! Well, luckily this time he didn't do any damage. I suggest you don't let him visit again!" Mr Simpson snapped, and stomped back down the garden path.

"Oh, Christy, he's really mean. I'm sorry for getting you into trouble!" Ellie said.

My Naughty Little Puppy

"Don't worry," Christy replied. "Mr
Simpson's always cross about something.
I kicked a ball over the fence last week, and
when he threw it back he'd put a message
on it in marker pen. It said next time he'd
'accidentally' dig into it with his garden fork!"

Ellie giggled. "He's horrible!"

Christy nodded and gave Ellie a hug.
"I think he likes being grumpy. He probably
enjoyed having the chance to tell us off!"

Chapter Eight

The Perfect Project

Ellie decided she'd better take Rascal home after that, in case he did anything else. She left Christy the paint, so she could spray their model and leave it to dry overnight. Then they planned to add the finishing touches after school the next day, so it would be ready to take in on Thursday morning.

"Did you manage to make something nice?" Mum asked when they arrived home. "And did Rascal behave?"

My Naughty Little Puppy

"Well ... we made a brilliant new model. But Rascal got a bit bored in Christy's garden and he went ... visiting."

"Oh, no! Not to Christy's grumpy next-door neighbour? Her mum's told me about him before."

"Yes," Ellie admitted. "But he didn't actually dig anything up!"

"That dog!" her mum muttered. "When we decided to get a Jack Russell, Ellie, nobody told me that they were known to be one of the stubbornest, hardest-to-train, generally naughty dogs there are."

"And the most gorgeous!" Ellie reminded her, holding Rascal up so he could nudge Mum's cheek with his damp little nose.

My Naughty Little Puppy

"Hmmm..." was all her mum said, but she did pat him.

"Actually, Mum, I think our new project is going to be better than the old one. The new design's really green and clever, and no one else will have anything like it," Ellie told her proudly. "Rascal did us a favour!"

Ellie was right. Mrs Harley was very impressed by their model on Thursday when they set it up on the project table at school.

"With a wind turbine? Very inventive, girls!" She made a little note in her folder.

Ellie and Christy grinned at each other. Their project definitely looked the best.

My Naughty Little Puppy

"And look, Sinead and Lily built a model of the same stadium we were making," Ellie pointed out. "So it's good that we did something different in the end."

Mr Turner arrived later that morning, and Mrs Harley showed him the projects. Everyone whispered excitedly, and Ellie and Christy both crossed their fingers.

My Naughty Little Puppy

"Well done, all of you. There were some really good ideas, but we've chosen Ellie and Christy's as the best project from this class." Mr Turner smiled at them. "A brilliant use of recycled materials, girls. We're going to put your model on display in the entrance hall, so the parents can all see it tomorrow."

"We should say thank you to Rascal for spoiling the old one!" Christy whispered, and Ellie nodded. Rascal really had done them a favour!

That afternoon they had a long Sports Day practice session, and Ellie felt like she must have tripped over at least a hundred hurdles.

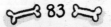

My Naughty Little Puppy

"Can't I just pretend to be ill tomorrow?" she muttered to Christy, but her friend shook her head firmly.

"No. Because you're going to be brilliant in the welly-throwing. You almost won when you had a go just now! Why don't you ask your mum if I can come over for a bit tonight, so we can do some more running practice without loads of people watching?"

"But people *will* be watching tomorrow!" Ellie pointed out.

Christy frowned. "Perhaps you could pretend you're invisible, or something?"

"I wish I was." Ellie sighed.

Christy rolled her eyes and pulled a face.

My Naughty Little Puppy

"All right," said Ellie. "I'll ask Mum if you can come over for one last practice."

"Run down to the end of the garden, touch the lilac tree and run back," Christy said.

"And try not to fall over your feet," Max added, poking his head round the kitchen door.

"That's mean!" Christy said.

"Yee-es," Max agreed. "But true."

"I bet I'm faster than you," Christy told Max, and he gave a disbelieving snort.

"Race you! Lilac tree and back – or are you too scared?"

Max smiled pityingly. "I'm two years older than you, and I'm a boy."

My Naughty Little Puppy

"Chicken," Christy teased.

Max shrugged. "OK. I could do with some practice for tomorrow, too. I was just warning you."

"She's really fast," Ellie told him. "She's going to win the hundred metres for our year, no problem."

Christy grinned at her, as she and Max lined up. Ellie sat down on the edge of the patio and hugged Rascal tightly, so he wouldn't try and join in. With her luck, he'd manage to trip Christy *and* Max up.

"Ready, steady, go!" Ellie yelled, and they shot off down the garden. They were neck and neck as they touched the lilac tree, but Max was taller and stronger, and he put on a huge burst of speed on the run back up the garden. There was no way he was going to be beaten by a girl. But he only *just* came first.

"Hey, you *are* good," he said admiringly.

"You – still – won!" Christy panted.

Max sat down next to Ellie. "I'm sorry. I shouldn't have teased you about Sports Day. You know what you should do?"

Ellie shook her head cautiously. She wasn't sure if Max was still teasing her.

"Practise the three-legged race with Christy. If you work out how to step together, you've got a really good chance. I'll show you, look."

He pulled Ellie to her feet, grabbed the skipping rope that was lying on the patio, and tied her and Christy's legs together. "You go middle, side, middle, side, and don't get mixed up. That's all there is to it."

Ellie looked at him doubtfully. It couldn't be that easy, could it? "Middle," she said slowly, and she and Christy put their tied feet forwards. Rascal trotted after them, looking confused.

"Say it together," Max told them.

"Middle, side, middle, side, middle, side," Ellie and Christy chanted, wobbling down the garden, and then they laughed out loud.

It worked!

"Told you so," Max said. "Rascal wants to join in, though. Maybe it ought to be a seven-legged race!"

Chapter Nine

Sports Day At Last

Ellie waved at Mum and Rascal, as her class walked out on to the school field. There were flags hung up all along the fence, and the mums and dads were sitting on rugs ready to watch the Sports Day events. Lots of little brothers and sisters were running around, and there were quite a few dogs, too.

Ellie's mum was sitting next to Christy's mum, with Christy's little sister Jade, but she hadn't brought Bouncer. Although Christy had begged for him to come, her mum had said Jade was quite enough to worry about, without a dog as well. Jade was playing with Rascal and seemed to be trying to put her comfort blanket on him as a cloak.

"Good afternoon, everyone! Welcome to Sports Day," Mr Turner announced over the PA system. "So that we have time to give everyone a chance at all the events, we'll be moving the classes around the field. Each class has been divided into four groups for most of the races."

He went on to read out a list of where all the different classes should be. Ellie's year were starting with the hurdles, Ellie's worst race. At least she was in the first six, so she could get it over with.

Please don't let me fall over, she whispered to herself, as Mrs Harley waved them off. It hadn't seemed to matter in the practices whether she went as fast as she could or slow and careful, she still tripped over the things.

My Naughty Little Puppy

So Ellie simply pretended she was racing across the park with Rascal, jumping over bits of long grass. It worked very well for the first four hurdles, but somehow the 'long grass' got twisted round her ankles on the last one, and she tumbled over.

Ellie clambered to her feet, scarlet-cheeked. She could hear all the mothers tutting and worrying if she was hurt. She jogged to the finish line, and slunk away to hide in a group of other girls from her class.

"Never mind." Christy gave her a hug. "Remember the welly-throwing. You'll be really good at that."

Ellie nodded gratefully. Just the skipping and the sack race to get through first. At least everybody fell over in that one...

My Naughty Little Puppy

Ellie lifted the red welly boot, and swung it gently back and forth. She grinned hopefully over at Mum and Rascal, who were standing close by, watching.

Rascal gave an excited bark and dragged on the lead to get closer to Ellie, but Mum pulled him back and got him to sit. Ellie watched proudly as Rascal sat down perfectly and lifted his nose to gobble up the treat Mum held out for him. He looked like an advert for puppy-training!

She shook herself firmly. She had to concentrate. Max had won three races already, and Christy had won the skipping race. Ellie at least wanted to get her welly

My Naughty Little Puppy

in the centre of the circle!

Ellie stepped up to the line and threw the welly. It was looking good! Surely that was going to go in...?

Then a small white-and-brown blur darted in front of her, and made a flying leap for the welly. It was a fantastic jump, even Ellie could see that, at the same time as she was squirming with embarrassment.

My Naughty Little Puppy

Rascal pranced over to her, tail wagging so fast it blurred, and laid the welly lovingly at her feet. It was the first time he'd ever given her anything he'd fetched, Ellie realized. She crouched down and gave him a pat as she took the welly.

Mum raced over and grabbed Rascal's lead. "Oh, Ellie, I'm sorry. He was sitting so nicely... I didn't notice he was about to chase the welly."

"Would you like another go?" Mrs Harley asked, as Ellie handed her the welly, but Ellie shook her head. All she wanted was to go and hide behind a tree at the far end of the field.

My Naughty Little Puppy

All of Ellie's class were jumping up and down and cheering. It was the final of the hundred metres for their year, and the competition was stiff. Ellie stood with her mum and Christy's mum, cheering Christy on.

"Look at that boy, he's so tall!" Christy's mum murmured, as Christy and the others lined up. "She can't possibly run faster than him."

But she could. Christy sped down the track, just beating the boy by a whisker. She danced over to them, beaming.

"Well done!" Ellie cried. "I told you you'd win."

Christy's mum gave her a hug. "That was brilliant! I'm so proud of you!"

Ellie saw her mum behind them, smiling,

My Naughty Little Puppy

and wished she'd won something. *I trained Rascal to fetch!* she told herself firmly. *That's really clever. And useful.*

"Mum, where's Jade?" Christy asked suddenly, and Christy's mum whirled round.

"She's sitting on the rug, isn't she?"

But, apart from Jade's little pink blanket lying there in a heap, the rug was bare.

Chapter Ten

Rascal the Hero

Christy's mum shook her head. "Jade was there a second ago," she said. "She was sitting there with her blanket. She can't just have disappeared..."

But she had. Christy's mum decided to stay by the blanket in case Jade came back, while Ellie's mum went to get Mr Turner to make an announcement over the PA system. Meanwhile, Christy and Ellie set off across the field to search for her.

My Naughty Little Puppy

Jade wasn't sitting with any of the other children scattered around the field, and she wasn't in the crowd watching the races.

"What about the cake stall?" Christy suggested, and she and Ellie tore across the field to check. But she wasn't there.

"Where else can we look?" Christy said, sounding panicky. She sometimes complained about how annoying Jade was, but she adored her really. It was like Ellie moaning about Max and Lila.

"We have a missing child, can everyone look out for Jade Lassiter, aged three. She must be somewhere on the field..." called Mr Turner, over the PA system.

Ellie swallowed. The announcement made it feel even more serious.

My Naughty Little Puppy

The races stopped, and people started searching all over the field. Where else was there to look?

"I know!" Ellie suddenly remembered a programme she'd watched about police dogs. She grabbed Christy's hand, and dragged her back to their rug.

"Jade's not here!" Christy protested. "What are you doing?"

"Getting this," Ellie answered, snatching up Jade's blanket. "Now we need Rascal."

Ellie's mum was comforting Christy's mum. "What do you want him for?" she asked, as Ellie tried to take Rascal's lead. "Ellie, this isn't the time..."

"Rascal can find her!" Ellie explained. "Look, Rascal." She held the pink blanket under his nose. "Jade carries this around all over the place, doesn't she? It'll smell of her," Ellie went on. "Rascal, where's Jade? Find Jade, Rascal."

Rascal sniffed at it with interest and looked up at Ellie, his eyes sparkling. He'd been bored, sitting around on the rug all afternoon, when there was a field he could have been chasing about in. Now Ellie was playing a good game.

My Naughty Little Puppy

He set off, looking this way and that, ears pricked and tail wagging. Ellie followed him, pulling Christy by the hand. "Good boy, Rascal. Keep going."

Rascal trotted across the field and round the corner of the school building.

"He can't be right, Ellie, there's nothing here," Christy murmured.

"He is leading us *somewhere*," Ellie told her. But even she was beginning to doubt Rascal, just a little bit.

Then Rascal stopped in front of the funny little metal shed where the sports equipment was kept. He looked up at Ellie, his tail wagging frantically.

"She's in there?" Ellie asked him, and Rascal pulled against his lead, dragging

My Naughty Little Puppy

her over to the door. Then he looked up again and barked loudly, almost as if he was saying, "There! Told you so!"

As Ellie opened the door, Rascal raced inside. At the back of the little shed, curled up on a pile of old gym mats, was Jade, holding on to the corner of a sack-race sack, instead of her beloved pink blanket.

"Hello, Rascal!" she said sleepily.

My Naughty Little Puppy

"You found her!" Christy squealed.
"Rascal, you clever, brilliant dog!"

Christy hared off at top speed, and
soon her mum and Ellie's mum and half the
school were all gathered round the shed.

"Ah, isn't she sweet?"

"And that clever dog found her?"

"You should be very proud of Rascal,
Ellie," Mrs Harley told her.

Christy's mum handed Ellie fifty pence.
"Once you've had your last race, go and
buy Rascal a reward from the cake stall. They
had some nice ham sandwiches earlier."

Ellie picked Rascal up. As she walked
back to the field, loads of people reached
out to pat him, like he was a hero. She felt
so proud she couldn't stop smiling.

My Naughty Little Puppy

"Are you ready?" Christy asked seriously. "Ellie, stop laughing! Remember, Max said we had to concentrate."

Ellie nodded, but she still had a silly smile on her face. She wasn't sure she could concentrate on the three-legged race. She didn't mind if she lost all the events now. Rascal was a hero, and he was hers!

"GO!"

"Middle, side, middle, side!" she and Christy muttered, and they stomped their way down the course, staying in rhythm.

Ellie risked a quick glance over her shoulder. They were winning! Max was

My Naughty Little Puppy

running alongside them, with Rascal safely on the lead. "Come on, Ellie, come on, Christy! You're nearly there!" he shouted.

But Jessie and Lydia were gaining on them. "Faster!" Christy hissed. "Middle, side, middle, side! Yes!"

They'd done it! She and Christy had actually won the three-legged race!

My Naughty Little Puppy

They collapsed in a giggling heap by the finishing line. Max dashed over and gave Ellie a lightning-fast hug, in case any of his friends noticed. "You did it!"

Mrs Harley laughed. "Well done, girls! That was the last race. Time to give out the prizes now."

"Excellent!" Christy grinned.

"Greedy! You've already won two races!" Ellie laughed. They stood listening to Mr Turner as he read out his long list of winners. All the way through Reception, Year One, Year Two...

"And in Year Four we have a special mention for Ellie Thomas, and an honorary member of the class, her dog, Rascal. Well done to Rascal for finding little Jade, who

was lost earlier on. Big clap for Rascal, please!"

Ellie's mum held him up, and Rascal barked with excitement.

"And I'm delighted to say that Ellie and Jade's big sister Christy have won the three-legged race. So well done to Ellie and Christy!"

As the list of races went on, Ellie cheered for Christy winning all those races, and Max winning practically everything in sight. She didn't mind at all. She had Rascal, and he was a rescue dog.

"Come on, let's go and buy him a sandwich!" Christy suggested.

The mums running the cake stall had heard all about Rascal, and insisted that

My Naughty Little Puppy

Ellie needed some fairy cakes for being so clever, and that Christy had better take some to cheer Jade up, too.

The girls raced back with their piled-up plates.

"Here you are, boy." Ellie tore the ham sandwich up into little pieces, and placed them on the paper plate. Rascal gulped them down delightedly, and then looked round, hoping for more.

"We should make him a medal," Christy's mum said.

Ellie laughed. "I think he'd rather just have another sandwich." And she picked him up, whispering, "I'll make you one at home. You're a star, Rascal!"

WOOF
magazine

Coming soon

It's Ellie's birthday soon, and she's planning a sleepover party. But her new friend Jess admits she is scared of dogs, and Rascal is sure to be very lively! Can Ellie and Rascal make it the best sleepover ever?

Q: My dog won't stop chewing our furniture and belongings. Help!
Annoyed Dog Owner

A: Your dog may be chewing things he shouldn't because he's bored, wants attention or misses you when you're out. Try these tips:

• Don't leave your belongings out where he can get to them, and use anti-chewing furniture sprays to put him off.

• Give him plenty of attention and exercise – he won't be such a nuisance if he's too tired to chew!

• Ask at your pet shop for toys and chews that are safe to leave with him. Don't give him old shoes because he'll confuse them with new ones!

• If you catch your dog chewing the wrong thing, interrupt him with a loud noise, or shouting, "No!" Remove the object, saying, "Give". Offer him a chew instead, praising him for taking it. Never shout at him *after* he's misbehaved, as he won't understand what he's being told off for!